Perfectly POPPY

The Summer Party

Written by Michele Jakubowski

Illustrated by Erica-Jane Waters

Raintree

Raintree is an imprint of Capstone Global Library Limited, a company incorporated in England and Wales having its registered office at 7 Pilgrim Street, London, EC4V 6LB – Registered company number: 6695582

www.raintreepublishers.co.uk
myorders@raintreepublishers.co.uk

Text © 2014 by Picture Window Books
First published in the United Kingdom in paperback in 2014
The moral rights of the proprietor have been asserted.

Designers: Heather Kindseth Wutschke, Kristi Carlson and Philippa Jenkins
Editor: Catherine Veitch
Originated by Capstone Global Library Ltd
Printed and bound in China

ISBN 978 1 406 28046 3 (paperback)
18 17 16 15
10 9 8 7 6 5 4 3 2

British Library Cataloguing in Publication Data
A full catalogue record for this book is available from the British Library.

Contents

Chapter 1
Party plans

"I can't wait for the party tonight!" Poppy said to her best friend, Millie.

"Me too," Millie agreed.

Every summer, the families in Poppy and Millie's village had a big outdoor party.

"I wonder what games we'll play this year?" Millie said.

Her favourite part of the party was playing games.

"I wonder what kind of food there will be?" Poppy said.

Her favourite part of the party was the food. In fact, her favourite part of every party was the food!

"We're going to bring s'mores,"

Millie said with a big smile.

"Snores?" Poppy asked.

"No, silly! S'mores," Millie said.

"My aunt from America makes them.

She roasts a marshmallow over a fire.

Then she puts it between biscuits and

a piece of chocolate."

Poppy loved anything with chocolate!

"They are so good you want to eat some more. Do you get it?" Millie asked. "S'more?"

"Oh, I get it," Poppy said. "And I can't wait to try one!"

Chapter 2

Heading for home

The party started at four o'clock and was in full swing by five. The garden looked great, and the weather was perfect. Everyone was having lots of fun.

Poppy's mum was busy, so Poppy decided to eat whatever she wanted. Her mum didn't even notice! She ate crisps, sweets and more crisps.

"Do you want some grapes?"

Millie asked.

"No thanks. I really like these

crisps," Poppy said.

"What about the s'mores later?"

Millie asked.

"I can eat those, too," Poppy said.

"Okay. But my dad says if you eat too much junk food you'll feel sick," Millie said.

"I'll be fine. Anyway, I'm full," Poppy said. "Let's watch television."

"I don't think so!" Millie said.

"The games are starting!"

"I'm tired," Poppy said.

"It's probably from eating so much

junk food," Millie said.

"No, it's not," Poppy said.

Just then, her older brother Nick came over.

"We're playing tag, and you're 'it'!" he cried, as he ran away.

Even though she was tired, Poppy jumped up. She didn't want to seem like a party pooper.

Poppy chased a lot of people and was glad when she finally tagged Emma.

After tag, everyone skipped. Then they had bike races.

"Let's play 'Home'! I'll be 'it'," Nick said.

Then he explained the rules.

A bucket was 'home'. The person

who was 'it' guarded the bucket.

Everyone had to hide. Then they

would run to kick the bucket,

shouting "Home!" as the person who

was 'it' tried to tag them.

Poppy frowned. She was really tired now, and her stomach hurt.

"What's wrong?" Millie asked.

"Nothing," Poppy lied. She didn't want Millie to know that she was right about eating all that junk food.

"Cheer up! After this game we will finally get our s'mores," Millie said.

Poppy tried to look excited, but it was hard.

"Hooray," she said quietly as she went to hide.

Chapter 3

S'more time

As Poppy sat behind a big tree, she decided to rest. She felt very smart. Nobody would even notice she wasn't playing the game.

Poppy heard Millie and James yell "Home!" They both got past Nick.

Poppy saw Jason on the other side of the garden. He looked like he was going to run for the bucket. Poppy knew that if Nick went after Jason, she could kick the bucket safely.

Sitting alone was boring. Her stomach still hurt, but she knew what she had to do. Maybe getting up and moving would help her feel better.

"Home!" she cried.

Poppy ran for the bucket as fast as she could. Nick wasn't fast enough to catch Jason and Poppy.

"Well done!" Millie said.

"Thanks," Poppy said. She was still tired, but sometimes tired felt good.

Poppy's mum called the children over for s'mores.

"Finally!" Millie said. "I bet you are super excited."

"Ummm . . . not really. I'm not very hungry," Poppy said.

"You never say that!" Millie said.

"I think I ate too much junk food," Poppy said.

"You really aren't going to have a s'more?" Millie asked.

"No. But I will be ready to have s'more fun once you have finished eating!" Poppy said.

"Very funny," said Millie, as she happily ate her treat.

"Funny and full," Poppy said with a smile. "What a day!"

Poppy's new words

I learned so many new words today! I wrote them down so that I could use them again.

agree share the same opinion or say yes

decide make up your mind to do something

explain make something easier to understand

guard protect or watch

party pooper person spoiling the fun at a party

probably almost certainly

Poppy's thoughts

After the big party I had some time to think. Here are some of my questions and thoughts from the day.

1. Did you know why I wasn't feeling good? Were there any clues in the story or illustrations?

2. When you go to a party, what is your favourite part? The food, games, or something else?

3. I learned a lesson about not eating too much junk food. Write about a time that you learned a lesson.

4. Write a story for a newspaper about our village party.

Kick the Can

We played a game called 'Home'. It's kind of like the game 'Kick the Can', which is also a lot of fun. Here are the rules:

1. Pick someone to be 'it'.

2. Place the can in the centre of your playing area (it can be a drinks can, a bucket, or anything else that you can kick).

3. The person who is 'it' closes his/her eyes and counts to twenty-five. During this time, everyone else runs and hides.

4. When the person who is 'it' sees someone hiding, they call out his/her name.

5. The hider and the 'it' person race back to the can.

6. If the 'it' person kicks the can first, the hider is put in jail. If the hider kicks the can first, anyone in jail is free and can hide again.

7. The 'it' person either counts again or keeps looking for more hiders, depending on who gets to the can first.

8. The game continues until everyone is found. The last person found is 'it' for the next game.

About the author

Michele Jakubowski grew up in Chicago, United States of America (USA). She has the teachers in her life to thank for her love of reading and writing. While writing has always been a passion for Michele, she believes it is the books she has read over the years, and the teachers who introduced them, that have made her the storyteller she is today. Michele lives in Ohio, USA, with her husband, John, and their children, Jack and Mia.

About the illustrator

Erica-Jane Waters grew up in the beautiful Northern Irish countryside, where her imagination was ignited by the local folklore and fairy tales. She now lives in Oxfordshire with her young family. Erica writes and illustrates children's books and creates art for magazines, greeting cards and various other projects.